Pop's Diner

JACK SHOLL

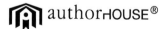 authorHOUSE®

AuthorHouse™ LLC
1663 Liberty Drive
Bloomington, IN 47403
www.authorhouse.com
Phone: 1-800-839-8640

Published by AuthorHouse   02/20/2014

ISBN: 978-1-4918-3922-5 (sc)
ISBN: 978-1-4918-3921-8 (e)

Library of Congress Control Number: 2013921168

FADE IN:

EXT. MANHATTAN SKYLINE—DAY

ZOOM in on SKYSCRAPER, and then on

An office window on a high floor.

INT. OFFICE BUILDING CORRIDOR—DAY

A SIGN behind a glass partition, where a receptionist sits behind a desk, reads: "Tectonics." EXECUTIVES, male and female in business attire, walk in and out of the doorway.

INT. OFFICE—DAY

Sitting in a large executive office are JOE BEASLEY, Chairman and CEO, 65, with a mane of white hair and pearly teeth; ROBBIE ARMSTRONG, 32; CAL CLEAVER, 28, company attorney; and BARNEY MCGEE, VP-Human Resources, 55, pudgy with a crew cut.

> BEASLEY
> Robbie, we think you're one heck of a guy. But the merger with Tungstron Electron has doubled up the staff. Tectonics doesn't need two Marketing heads. We've discussed it, and we are terminating you.

> MCGEE
> In other words, you're excess. Of course, you'll get a severance payment.

ROBBIE

I've worked for the company since I graduated from school. My performance record is better than anybody's. Our growth figures prove it.

BEASLEY

Thing's have changed since the merger, Robbie.

ROBBIE

So, who's taking my place?

MCGEE

Taylor Stinson.

ROBBIE

Taylor Stinson? The son of Wade Stinson, Tungstron Electron
Chairman?
    (Pause)
You sold me out as part of the merger.
Sold isn't the right word. You're dumping me like a bag of garbage.

CLEAVER

I'd watch what you were saying, Robbie. Words like that won't get you very far. You don't want us to sue you for libel on top of everything else, do you?

BEASLEY

Hold on, Cal.

MCGEE
Stop by at my office on your way out, Robbie, and we'll give you your severance check.

Robbie gets up and storms out the door.

Beasley flashes a toothy smile.

BEASLEY
Have a nice day!

INT. OUTER OFFICE—CONTINUING

Robbie slams the door to Beasley's office behind him.

TAYLOR STINSON, 32, with large buck teeth and ears and plastered-down yellow hair with a cowlick sticking up, is at the SECRETARY's desk. Stinson is dressed in an overly starched and pressed gray business suit, yellow tie and matching yellow pocket handkerchief.

SECRETARY
Mr. Beasley will see you, now, Mr. Stinson.

Robbie passes them by, rolls his eyes and exits.

INT. OFFICE BUILDING CORRIDORS—CONTINUING

Robbie strides straight ahead. He passes OFFICE BOYS, MESSENGERS, SECRETARIES, EXECUTIVES, CLERKS in cubicles. Robbie ignores them all.

ROBBIE'S OUTER OFFICE

Robbie walks past his SECRETARY, a brunette in her 50s.

The secretary gets up and follows Robbie through the door into his office.

Robbie is already on his way back out.

> SECRETARY
> What about your stuff?

> ROBBIE
> Leave it.

> SECRETARY
> But your boat photo? You loved that so much.

> ROBBIE
> Just a dream, Meg. In the four year's I've had it, I've used it once. Throw it out, or leave it. I don't care.

Robbie exits.

INT. TRAIN CAR—AFTERNOON

Robbie, his necktie loosened at the collar, stares out the window.

EXT. TRAIN STATION—AFTERNOON

Robbie gets off the train.

Robbie walks to the parking lot of the train station.

Robbie gets in a silver Porsche.

The Porsche SCREECHES out of the parking lot.

EXT. ARMSTRONG HOUSE—AFTERNOON

The house is a very large, tudor-style, executive home in the New York City suburb of Bronxville.

The Porsche ROARS into the driveway.

Robbie exits the Porsche and SLAMS the door.

Robbie walks up the front steps of the house. Robbie opens the door.

INT. ARMSTRONG HOUSE FOYER—CONTINUING

GLORIA ARMSTRONG, a lithe blonde in her early 30s, is on her way out the door with a suitcase.

> ROBBIE
> Where are you going?

> GLORIA
> I'm leaving. For good. I've had it. I'm getting a divorce. You're a workaholic. You're never home. I'm going to my mother's. You'll hear from my attorney.

> ROBBIE
>
> You've never complained before.

Gloria steps by him and opens the door.

> ROBBIE
> (continuing)
> Is there someone else?

Gloria stops.

A beat.

Gloria turns to Robbie.

> GLORIA
>
> As a matter of fact, yes, there is, Robbie.
> Goodbye.

Gloria SLAMS the door behind her.

EXT. TRAIN STATION—CAFÉ—MORNING

Robbie, in sweat shirt and baseball jacket, jeans and sneakers with a stubble of beard, reads a newspaper.

WILLY, WALTER, BRAD AND CHARLEY have pulled up chairs around the table, filled with bagels and danish on paper plates next to white styrofoam cups of steaming coffee.

They all read the morning newspapers.

WALTER

See anything in the Want Ads?

CHARLEY

Nothing that wasn't there yesterday. Unless
you want a job grooming dogs.

WALTER

No, thanks. I have a hard enough time
grooming myself these days.

SAM BIXBY, mid-30's, dressed for work in gray suit, yellow
suspenders, and carrying a brown leather attaché case, comes by.

SAM

Hi, fellows! Who won the game last night?

ROBBIE

Mets.

SAM

I haven't looked at the paper yet.
How's Apex Pharmaceuticals doing?

Willy opens his newspaper to the stock page.

WILLY

Low price.

SAM

Just keep watching. We're expecting to hear
from the FDA tomorrow on approval of our
next big drug.

The commuter train SCREECHES to a halt at the station platform.

                    SAM
                 (continuing)
        Gotta go!

                    SAM
              (continuing; smiling)
        See you retirees later!

                   ROBBIE
        See you, Sam!

                    BRAD
        You hear what he said.

                   WILLY
        About Apex, you mean?

                    BRAD
        Yeah, sounds like a sure thing. A person
        could make a lot of money on what he just
        said.

                   ROBBIE
        Isn't that inside information?

                    BRAD
        That's the whole point.

                   ROBBIE
        So you make a few bucks. So what?

BRAD

No, I mean a killing. I got a great idea. We're all hurting for money. I mean, Charley, you're about to be evicted, and my unemployment's running out. Why don't we pool all the money we've got left and buy a big chunk of stock?

WILLY

We split the proceeds?

BRAD

You got it.

WILLY

What do you say, fellas?

BRAD

I'm in. You Charley?

CHARLEY

Yep.

BRAD

Walter?

WALTER

I'm in.

BRAD

Robbie?

                    ROBBIE
Why not. I've got nothing to do, anyway.

                     BRAD
You collect the money from everyone. Then buy
a big block on—line on your brokerage account.
And we'll double that by buying on margin.

                    WILLY
It's a sure thing. We can't lose.

INT. TRAIN STATION—MORNING

WILLY, WALTER, BRAD AND CHARLEY, styrofoam
coffee cups on the table, have the morning newspapers in
front of them.

                   CHARLEY
Who ever could have imagined?

                     BRAD
The FDA asked for more testing.

                    WALTER
The stock's down fifty percent.

                    WILLY
Maybe it'll go back up?

                   CHARLEY
Not fast enough. Remember we bought on
margin. The margin calls will wipe us out. I
hate to say it, guys, we're wiped out.

INT. MANHATTAN LAW OFFICE—DAY

Robbie sits across from attorney SAUL ARBRAMOVITZ in Abramovitz's book-lined office.

> SAUL
> So, that leaves you with three hundred and seventy-seven dollars and twenty-three cents.

> ROBBIE
> Just make it three-hundred and seventy-seven even, Saul. You can keep the change.

> SAUL
> Your generosity knows no bounds.

Saul gives Robbie a check.

EXT. BANK—DAY

Robbie counts money and puts the bills in his pocket.

EXT. MANHATTAN STREET—DAY

Robbie walks down Seventh Avenue, past electronic stores, deli's, convenience stores and food markets. PEOPLE and a MESSENGER on a bicycle hurry by.

EXT. PORT AUTHORITY—DAY

Robbie enters the bustling bus terminal, streaming with PEOPLE.

INT. TICKET WINDOW—CONTINUING

> ROBBIE
>
> I'd like a ticket.

> CASHIER
>
> Where to?

> ROBBIE
>
> Anywhere?

> CASHIER
>
> Well, look, now, I've got to have a place.

> ROBBIE
>
> Where would you go?

> CASHIER
>
> Tahiti, but that doesn't matter. Anywhere but here.

> ROBBIE
>
> Give me an idea.

> CASHIER
>
> Here's a timetable. But there's a thousand places.

> ROBBIE
>
> I figure I can spend a hundred and twenty—five dollars. Where will that get me?

> CASHIER
>
> One-way or round-trip?

> ROBBIE
>
> One way.

The cashier consults a schedule.

> CASHIER
>
> Looks to me like that'll get you as far as
> Vistulia, Iowa.

> ROBBIE
>
> Give me a ticket.

EXT. HIGHWAY INTERSECTION—NIGHT

A Greyhound bus comes to a halt.

Robbie exits the bus. Robbie is still dressed in his business suit, although he's removed his necktie.

The bus drives off, leaving Robbie standing at the empty intersection.

Robbie walks to an all-night restaurant and bar next to a truck stop and gas station.

INT. BAR—NIGHT

Robbie enters.

A dozen other MEN, mostly truckers in jeans and sporting tattoos, are at the bar.

Robbie takes a seat at the bar, next to two young toughs, MARIO and AXEL, in jeans and black, leather jackets.

The BARTENDER comes over to Robbie.

> BARTENDER
>
> What'll you have?

> ROBBIE
>
> A draft beer.

> BARTENDER
>
> What kind?

> ROBBIE
>
> Any kind'll do. I've been on that bus for
> days.

The bartender pulls a beer from the tap and puts it in front of Robbie.

Robbie drinks the glass of beer half down.

> ROBBIE
>
> (continuing)
>
> Aaaahhhh!!!

> AXEL
>
> Where you headed, buddy?

ROBBIE

Nowhere. I mean here. This is the end of the
line for me.

AXEL

You live here?

ROBBIE

Nope. Going to get a place to stay in town
and a job.

MARIO

You got a car?

ROBBIE

Nope. Guess I'll walk.

MARIO

Come on. We'll give you a ride into town.
We were just leaving, anyway. Right, Axel?

ROBBIE

That's mighty kind of you.

Mario, Axel and Robbie get up from the bar.

Mario, Axel and Robbie exit.

INT. PICKUP TRUCK—CONTINUING

The pickup truck bounces down the road. Robbie sits in the
middle of the seat between Axel at the wheel and Mario.
Heavy metal MUSIC plays on the radio.

> MARIO
> (to Robbie)

Nice suit.

> ROBBIE

Thanks. Needs a good pressing, though.

> MARIO

Must of cost a lot?

> ROBBIE

Custom made.

> MARIO

I'm going to buy a custom-made suit myself.

Mario opens the glove compartment. Mario takes out a heavy metal wrench.

Mario hits Robbie over the head with the wrench.

> MARIO
> (continuing)

With what you've got in your pockets!

EXT. ROADSIDE—NIGHT

The red pickup truck is stopped.

The truck door opens.

Mario gets out of the truck.

Mario pulls an unconscious Robbie from the truck and throws him on the ground.

Mario and Axel go through Robbie's pockets.

Mario takes Robbie's wallet.

Axel takes Robbie's watch off his wrist.

Axel and Mario get back in the truck.

The truck ROARS off.

Robbie lays unconscious in the dirt at the edge of the road.

FADE TO:

EXT. ROADSIDE—DAY

ROBBIE'S P.O.V.—A DEVIL'S FACE

> SKYE (V.O.)
> Aye there, mate. What's up. Too much to drink last night?

A giant bus is to the side of the road. The bus is painted bright colors all over and a SIGN on the side reads: "HOUNDS OF HADES. WORLD TOUR."

INT. BUS—DAY

The bus has a refrigerator, bar and kitchen. On one side there is a bookshelf.

SKYE STONE, mid-20's, the leader of the band, hands Robbie a cup of coffee. Skye, a young cheerful fellow, has removed the Devil's face mask, which sits on the seat next to him.

Robbie gets up and stretches.

Robbie looks at the titles of the books on the bookshelf: Heidegger, the Dali Lama, Kant, Schopenhauer, Stephen Hawking, Bertrand Russell.

> ROBBIE
>
> Impressive collection. For a traveling rock band.

> SKYE
>
> Don't let the costumes fool you, Mate. I got my Ph.D. in philosophy from Cambridge. LOUIE's got a degree in mathematics, and STANLEY used to be a Jesuit priest. The costumes are so we can relate to the culture, the people, as they say, 'bro.

> ROBBIE
>
> I thought about studying philosophy when I was in school. I should have. I'd have been better off than in the business world.

RITCHIE is at the wheel of the bus.

RICHIE

The radio says "Tribute to the Void" is the number one song in the country and on its way to being an all-time best seller.

SKYE

(to Robbie)

I knew it. They didn't want to stop for you. But I insisted. You're my good luck charm, Mate.

EXT. HIGHWAY INTERSECTION—DAY

The bus is stopped.

Robbie and Skye get off the bus.

Robbie's unsteady on his feet. He has a large bandage on his head. He's unshaven and looks terrible.

SKYE

Sorry we can't take you the whole way to town, Mate. But we gotta make tracks to our next gig, I mean engagement.

ROBBIE

Well, thanks for picking me up.

SKYE

No problem.

Skye digs his hand into his pocket and pulls out a small roll of bills. Skye counts the bills and gives thm to Robbie.

SKYE

(continuing)

A hundred dollars. That's all I got, Mate. We don't carry much cash with us when we're on the road. Get yourself something to eat.

ROBBIE

Thanks. I'll pay you back. Someday.

Skye hands Robbie a little white business card.

SKYE

Take this too. In case you ever need anything, let me know. Remember, you're my good luck charm!

Robbie looks at the card. The card READS: "Hounds of Hades, 3023 Wilshire Boulevard, Beverly Hills, CA, 21202. Phone: 310-868-942."

Skye gets back in the bus.

The band members wave out the window to Robbie as the bus pulls away.

EXT. INTERSECTION—DAY

Robbie walks to a McBurger Palace fast-food restaurant.

Robbie enters.

INT. MCBURGER PALACE—DAY

The restaurant is full of TRAVELERS.

KATIE JOHNSON, in a McBurger outfit, takes orders and slings burgers, fries and cokes.

Robbie stands in line. He looks at the plastic menu atop the serving counter.

> KATIE
>
> And what will you have?

Robbie stares at Katie. Katie's very cute. Robbie's mesmerized.

> KATIE
> (continuing)
> It's not as though there's a lot to choose from on the menu.

> ROBBIE
> Give me a giant double McBurger and a cup of coffee.

Robbie stares at Katie as she gets a wrapped burger from the counter behind her and pours a paper cup of coffee from an aluminum coffee dispenser.

Katie places the burger and coffee cup on a plastic tray on the counter in front of Robbie.

Robbie drops three dollar bills and some change on the counter.

> KATIE
> Sugar and cream over there on the counter.

> ROBBIE
>
> You have any job openings here?

> KATIE
>
> Nope. If there were any jobs around this burg, I wouldn't be here. You've got to be kidding. Try in town.

Katie signals to the next patron.

> KATIE
> (continuing)
>
> Next.

Robbie takes his tray and sits down at an empty table. Robbie eats his burger as he watches Katie serve CUSTOMERS.

EXT. TOWN—MORNING

An old, battered pickup truck stops in front of a diner on the main street of the town. A sign on top of the diner READS: "Pop's Diner."

Robbie gets out of the pickup truck.

Robbie waves to the DRIVER. The pickup truck clambers off.

EXT. POP'S DINER—DAY

Robbie enters the diner.

INT. POP'S DINER—DAY

Two dozen booths ring the perimeter, by the front window and the walls. A serving counter with twelve seats is to the rear. A dozen tables with red dull red formica tops are in the center. A few PEOPLE sit at the counter.

MOM, with white hair, is behind the counter. Mom cuts a slice of pie on a plate under a plastic cover.

Robbie sits down at the counter.

> MOM
> What'll you have, son?

> ROBBIE
> Guess you could give me a cup of coffee.

Robbie looks around the diner.

Mom brings a cup of coffee. Mom puts the cup in front of Robbie.

> ROBBIE
> (continuing)
> Thanks. Say, you wouldn't know where a man could get a job?

> MOM
> Son, that's the question everybody around here asks. There isn't one to be had til you get to the state capitol. And then I'm not so sure. Times are tough.

ROBBIE

Could you use someone here? Anything?

Mom turns to the opening between the counter and the kitchen.

MOM

Pop, could you come out here for a moment?

POP, in his 60's, a white apron around his waist, comes around the corner from behind the back counter.

MOM
(continuing)
Man here asks if we need anybody?

ROBBIE

I really need a job. Anything. And a place to stay. I'm really in a jam. I lost my job and my wife and I got robbed. I've got nothing.

MOM

Looks like a nice young man, Pop. Kind of reminds me of when you were young.

POP

Well, I guess we can use someone around here. The dishwasher quit last week. Not that I can blame him. Can't pay much of anything way business is.

ROBBIE

I'd be obliged for anything.

                    POP

Well, OK. You can sleep out in the shed
behind the house. It's got a bed and running
water. Mom's brother used to live there, til
the war. We'll take out what you eat from
your pay. Not that it's going to be much.

Robbie shakes Pop's hand.

                  ROBBIE

Thanks! Robbie Armstrong is my name.
Believe me, you won't regret it. What do I
call you?

Pop scratches his head.

                    POP

My real name is Fauntnelroy Googenheim.
My wife's name is Gesthelme—Gesthelme
Googenheim. You can just call us Mom and
Pop, like everybody else. It's easier.

                  ROBBIE

OK. Mom and Pop. I like the sound of it.
My own parents are retired in Arizona.

INT. DINER—KITCHEN—DAY

Robbie washes dishes. A DOG, a shaggy
mutt, lays on the floor by Robbie's feet.

> ROBBIE
> (to dog)
> How easily we fall from grace. One day
> you're on top. The next on the bottom. It's
> all so fragile.

The dog rolls his eyes upward, listening attentively and sympathetically.

> ROBBIE
> (continuing)
> From the big time to this.

INT. SHED—DAY

Robbie washes himself from a small sink. He shaves and restores himself to his normal appearance.

EXT. TOWN—MAIN STREET—DAY

Robbie walks down the main street of the small town. He walks past a hardware store, a movie theatre, a drug store, a barber shop, an auto garage, a stationery store, a post office, a realtor, and a five-and-dime store.

Robbie stops in front of the five-and-dime.

EXT. FIVE AND DIME STORE—DAY

Robbie enters.

Robbie walks through the narrow aisles, filled with small bins of various little toys and candies.

Robbie stops in front of a bin. Robbie takes out a harmonica and looks at it.

Robbie blows into the harmonica. The harmonica makes a SOUND.

An ELDERLY WOMAN behind the cash register looks up. The woman gives him an amused look.

Robbie takes the harmonica to the counter and gives the woman two quarters.

Robbie exits the store.

EXT. STREET—DAY

Katie walks out of the stationery store.

Katie reads the <u>Wall Street Journal</u> as she walks.

Robbie walks out of the five-and-dime store.

Robbie collides with Katie, who's not looking where she's going. Katie drops the newspaper on the ground, the sheets of newspaper scattering about.

ROBBIE
Whoooaaa! Excuse me.

KATIE
I'll say. Why don't you look where you're going!

> ROBBIE
>
> I sort of think it's the other way around. I
> mean you were looking at that newspaper.

> KATIE
>
> Of course I was, you jerk. It's not as though
> this is Grand Central Station.

> ROBBIE
>
> OK, I'm sorry. Here let me get your paper
> for you.

Robbie bends down and picks up the scattered sheets of newspaper.

Robbie hands the newspaper to Katie.

> ROBBIE
> (continuing)
> The Wall Street Journal?

> KATIE
>
> Yes. I can read, too.

> ROBBIE
>
> I haven't seen one of those in weeks. Where
> did you get it?

Katie looks at Robbie with curiosity. Katie jerks her head to the side over her shoulder.

KATIE

Stationery store, over there. It's a week old.
But that's better than nothing, I suppose.

ROBBIE

I don't suppose I could borrow that for a
second and look at the stock tables?

KATIE

Go get your own.

Katie flippantly walks down the street.

ROBBIE

OK. I will!

Katie stops. Katie turns.

Robbie walks toward the stationery store.

KATIE

Wait a minute!

Robbie turns.

Katie walks up to him.

KATIE
(continuing)
Sorry. That wasn't very nice of me.

Katie hands Robbie the newspaper.

ROBBIE

Thanks.

Robbie opens the newspaper, and glances inside.

KATIE

Weren't you in McBurger a week or two ago?
You had a big bump on your head.

Robbie looks up from the paper.

ROBBIE

Yes. I guess I was. I just arrived here.

KATIE

I thought that was you. You look a lot better
than you did then.

ROBBIE

It's a long story. How's life at McBurger
Palace?

KATIE

It's a long story.

Robbie hands the paper back to Katie.

ROBBIE

Thanks. You'll have to tell it to me.

KATIE

Maybe. Sometime.

ROBBIE

Say, do you like ice cream?

KATIE

Sure.

ROBBIE

I have an idea. Let's go over to Pop's diner
and have a dish. Pop makes the best vanilla
ice cream I've ever tasted.

KATIE

I've really got to go.

ROBBIE

Come one. There's not much to do around
here. And if I treat you to some ice cream,
maybe you'll let me read some more of your
paper.

Katie laughs.

KATIE

Sure. OK. Why not?

INT. DINER—CONTINUING

Robbie and Katie enter the diner. Mom is behind the counter.

Robbie and Katie sit in a booth by the window.

Mom approaches the table.

ROBBIE

Two dishes of your best vanilla ice cream.

MOM

How're you, Katie? Haven't seen you in a while.

KATIE

Been busy. Working at the McBurger.

MOM

How's business there? I hear it's good.

KATIE

If you like stuffing yourself with grease for five minutes and then hitting the road, I guess it's OK.

MOM

Two vanilla ice creams.

ROBBIE

You know each other?

KATIE

Yes, stupid. Everyone in a small town knows one another. Don't you know that?

ROBBIE

What's a girl like you, doing in a place like this?

                    KATIE
I was born and raised here. Til I went off
school.

Mom brings two dishes of vanilla ice cream to the table.

                    MOM
Robbie, when you're done socializing, maybe
you could socialize a little with those dishes
in the back. They've been piling up since
breakfast.

Katie looks at Robbie with surprise.

                    ROBBIE
OK, Mom.

Robbie turns back to Katie.

                    ROBBIE
                 (continuing)
So, why did you come back?

                    KATIE
Like I said, it's a long story. After I
graduated from college, I went off to the
big city, and got a big job. Then, it all fell
to pieces. I lost my job in the big dot.com
blowout.

                    ROBBIE
You ever hear of Tectonics?

KATIE

Of course. Who hasn't?

ROBBIE

You're looking at the former, and I emphasize former, chief marketing officer.

Katie's eyes open wide.

ROBBIE

(continuing)

You and I seem to be in the same boat. Rather, in the same canoe, downstream without a paddle.

KATIE

I was the head of marketing. Big corner office. The big allure, of course, was stock options. Now they're worth nothing. I'm out of job. I'm out of money. The market's dried up. So, I decided to come home. And reevaluate my life.

ROBBIE

I can hardly say serving burgers at McBurger is undertaking a serious reevaluation of your life.

KATIE

A dishwasher hardly has room to talk.

Katie gets up.

KATIE
(continuing)
Thanks for the ice cream.

Katie turns and throws Robbie the newspaper.

KATIE
(continuing)
And, yes, here. You can keep the paper.

Katie exits.

INT./ EXT. DINER

Robbie watches Katie through the window of the diner as Katie bounces off down the street.

INT. SHED—EVENING

Robbie sits on the side of the small bed.

Robbie plays the harmonica to the dog.

The dog HOWLS and wags its tail.

ROBBIE
What a fine kettle of fish. Here's a guy who can't take a girl anywhere because he's got no money.

INT. MCBURGER PALACE—EVENING

The restaurant is full of TRAVELERS.

Katie slings burgers onto plastic trays, and rings up the cash register.

Katie looks up.

Katie's P.O.V.—Robbie is at the head of the line. Robbie smiles.

> KATIE
> Your usual? Double McBurger. With a dash of sarcasm?

> ROBBIE
> No. The only thing I want is to ask if after work, you'll go out with me?

> KATIE
> Like where? There's no place to go?

> ROBBIE
> We'll take a walk.

Katie hesitates.

A FAT MAN, holding a baby in one arm and a small boy with the other hand, is behind Robbie in line.

> FAT MAN
> Go ahead! Take a walk with him. And then you can take my order.

> KATIE
> OK.

FAT MAN
That's more like it. Four McBurgers, four big fries, three strawberry milkshakes, one chocolate milkshake.

Robbie stands to the side of the line of CUSTOMERS.

Robbie waves to Katie, who spins about behind the counter and grabs paper-wrapped burgers from the kitchen portal.

EXT. MCBURGER PALACE—EVENING

The lights are half-on in the empty restaurant. Inside, through the window, the MANAGER moves a table about.

Katie walks across the parking lot with one car in it.

Robbie stands at the edge of the parking lot.

ROBBIE
Hi!

KATIE
Hi!

EXT. COUNTRY ROAD—EVENING

Robbie and Katie walk along the road. Crickets and cicadas CHIRP.

ROBBIE
It's no fun being broke. But, there is a compensation.

> ### KATIE
>
> What's that?

> ### ROBBIE
>
> It's peaceful.

Robbie takes Katie's hand as they stroll.

EXT. HILLTOP—EVENING

Robbie and Katie stand at the top of the hill overlooking the lights of the town.

> ### ROBBIE
>
> I forgot who I was. For the first time since I was a child I can smell the rain, the grass, the air.

> ### KATIE
>
> Look.

Stars SPARKLE in the black sky among scattered onrushing clouds.

> ### ROBBIE
>
> Beautiful. There's the Big Dipper. I've flown a million miles—from here to China and back dozens of time—and never once saw the Big Dipper.

RAIN begins to fall.

Robbie takes Katie in his arms. They embrace. Robbie kisses Katie. She responds.

The shower clears. Both are wet.

(O.S.) BRRRUUUPPPPPP! BRRRRUUUUPPPP!
BRRRUUUPPP!

> KATIE
>
> What's that?

> ROBBIE
>
> Bullfrogs in the old pond.

EXT. POND—NIGHT

A glistening white, full moon is reflected in the watery pool, surrounded by bulrushes. Lily pads float here and there on the tranquil surface.

> ROBBIE
>
> Look!

A large BULLFROG sits on a lily pad, CROAKING.

> KATIE
>
> He's cute.

> ROBBIE
>
> Let's see if we can catch one.

> KATIE
>
> That's mean.

ROBBIE
No, it's fun. We won't keep it. We'll let it go.

Robbie and Katie splash about the pond, trying to catch FROGS with their hands.

Robbie and Katie fall in the swamp, LAUGHING.

Robbie and Katie kiss, again.

INT. DINER—DAY

Robbie and Katie are in a booth. Robbie and Katie drink coffee and read newspapers.

ROBBIE
I've been thinking. With all the energy and talents we've been putting into washing dishes, sweeping up and slinging burgers, if we put the same energy into something else that pays well, we could make a fortune.

KATIE
I thought that's just what you didn't want. That's what caused all the trouble in the first place: working all the time. Being a slave to the workplace and job. No time to think, reflect, relax. It's an extraordinary price to pay. I thought you wanted to give that all up?

ROBBIE
I did. I do. I was just saying, that's all.

Pop enters. Pop wears an old sports coat over his kitchen khakis.

KATIE

Hi, Pop.

MOM

How are you doing, Katie? Robbie?

ROBBIE

Just fine.

POP

Wish I could say the same.

KATIE

What's the matter?

POP

Just came from the bank. Curt Tyson's rasing the rent and I just went over to see Weatherby. There's nothing else he can do. We're already way overextended. The economy's bad and those places out on the freeway are taking all our business.

KATIE

There must be some way. Maybe if you talked to Tyson.

POP

No, that'll do no good. He's been wanting to start a gun and ammo store here for a long time. We're the only place in town that doesn't own our property.

ROBBIE
Why can't Tyson open up his store on the freeway, like everybody else?

POP
There's a restriction on having that type of business visible on the interstate. No, I don't see any way out. I was hoping to put enough away to send Luther and Tess to state college, but I don't see how that's going to be possible. What with Mom's medical bills for her arthritis. I'm going to just pack it all up, I guess. You got any jobs out there at the McBurger, Katie?

KATIE
Nope. Not unless you want mine.

Pop goes behind the counter, takes off his jacket and puts on a cook's apron.

Katie looks at Pop.

Katie looks at Robbie.

KATIE
(continuing)
Do you think?

A beat.

> ROBBIE

Think what?

> KATIE

That we could help Pop? After all, you and I know enough about running and growing businesses. A little restaurant should be a cinch.

EXT. DINER—NIGHT

Sign in window: "CLOSED"

INT. DINER—NIGHT

Robbie is on a ladder. Dropcloths hang over the tables, booths and counter.

> KATIE

How's it going?

> ROBBIE

Fresh coat of paint will do miracles. What's that?

> KATIE

The marketing plan. I finished it last night.

> ROBBIE

Let's see.

Robbie and Katie sit on the bottom rung of the ladder. Robbie and Katie look over the open black binder of the marketing plan book.

ROBBIE
(continuing)
This is pretty extensive and ambitious.

KATIE
So, what's wrong with that, hot shot?

ROBBIE
If you were going to open a new chain of restaurants to compete with McBurgers, that's one thing. But we're just trying to help Pop enter the 21st Century.

KATIE
Come on, Robbie! Get with the program!

EXT. DINER—DAY

PEOPLE walk by the front of the diner. Robbie's on the roof.

Robbie hangs a new, modern "Pop's Diner" SIGN over the front of the diner, atop the front window.

Katie, in blue jeans and T-shirt, is in the middle of the Street. Katie signals Robbie to move the sign right, and then left, and then to the center.

EXT. POP'S HOUSE—DAY

Katie, in sweatsuit and sneakers, walks along the worn, white, wooden picket fence that lines the flowers and shrubbery of the grassy yard in front of the old, wooden, Victorian house.

INT. POP'S HOUSE—DINNING ROOM—DAY

Luther, 14, and Tess, 12, work at a laptop computer and printer on the old, wooden dinning room table.

Katie enters.

> KATIE
> How's my computer working out?

> LUTHER
> This is really cool!

> TESS
> It does so many things!

Luther prints out a colored, paper menu.

Katie takes the menu from the printer.

The MENU has has a DRAWING of August Foliage on it.

Katie reads the menu aloud.

> KATIE
> Mom's Meat Loaf. Pop's Open-Faced Roast
> Beef Sandwich. Mississippi Mud Pie. She-
> Devil Crab Cakes. Luther must have named
> those after you, Tess.

TESS

Giggles.

KATIE

A traditional, all-American menu. Perfect.

INT. DINER KITCHEN—NIGHT

Robbie, at the table, looks over a pile of old, battered <u>House Beautiful</u> and <u>Better Homes and Gardens</u> magazines. The dog is on Robbie's lap.

Dishes, pots and pans are piled high in the sink.

EXT. FIELD—DAY

Robbie and Katie sit in shade of an old chestnut tree. A blanket is spread on the ground. A wicker picnic basket is on the blanket.

Robbie and Katie eat sandwiches and drink cans of soda.

KATIE

You make a mean peanut butter and jelly sandwich.

ROBBIE

Haven't had one of these since I was six years old.

Robbie reaches over and wipes jelly from Katie's chin.

Robbie hands Katie half of another sandwich.

                    ROBBIE
                (continuing)
        Here, try this one. I added mashed banana,
        it's great.

(S.O.) A LOUD ROARING of ENGINES and WHOOPING
and HOLLERING.

                    KATIE
        What one earth is that?

Robbie and Katie stand up.

Robbie and Katie's P.O.V.—A short rotund man, CURT
TYSON, in fox hunting garb—red cap and vest, white
breeches and boots—bounces over the countryside atop a
Harley motorcycle hog. Tyson has two ammo belts strapped
across his chest over the riding habit and a double-barreled
shotgun in one hand.

Tyson, along with SIX other MEN on motorcycles similarly
garbed, pursue a brown FOX.

Tyson fires a BLAST from his shotgun.

                    KATIE
                (continuing)
        They're trying to kill the fox!

The fox, way in the lead of the motorcycles, runs toward Katie
and Robbie.

The fox dashes into a clump of bushes behind the tree where Katie and Robbie stand.

Tyson and the group of motorcyclists ROAR up to Robbie and Katie.

> TYSON
> Excuse us. But did you see a fox go by?

> ROBBIE
> Yes.

Robbie points in the opposite direction, away from the bush.

> TYSON
> Much obliged.

Tyson REVS the motorcycle engine.

Tyson turns to BART CHISOLM, a scrawny man with a thin beard.

> TYSON
> (continuing)
> Let's get going. That fox isn't going to outfox us!

> CHISOLM
> Its tail is going to look mighty pretty on the radio antenna of my car.

> TYSON
> Yeeehaaah!

Tyson and the motorcyclists ROAR off in the opposite direction.

The fox peers out of the brush.

Robbie and Katie walk over to the fox's hideout in the bushes.

Robbie pushes aside a few branches.

Robbie and Katie's P.O.V.—Inside the den of the bushes, the fox nuzzles SEVERAL baby foxes.

                    KATIE
        They're so cute!

Robbie and Katie smile at one another.

EXT. DINER—MORNING

Pop stands in front of the diner looking at the new sign and the spruced up front.

Pop picks up some mail on the ground at the door of the diner. Pop takes a key out of his pocket and opens the door to the diner. He enters the diner.

INT. DINER-CONTINUING

Pop takes a key out of his pocket and opens the door to the diner. He enters the diner.

Pop's P.O.V.—The diner is completely refurbished. Pots of flowers and plants are on the floors and counters. New pictures of flowers and landscapes hang on the freshly painted walls. The counters and booths sparkle. A homey look has transformed the old, tired, worn-down appearance of the diner.

Pop stares in amazement.

> ROBBIE (O.S.)
> What do you think?

Pop turns to see a beaming Robbie and Katie.

> POP
> I don't know how I'll ever pay you back.

> ROBBIE
> Don't worry about it, Pop. You took a chance on me. We're just trying to help pay you back.

EXT. STREET—DAY

Katie leans in the shade against an old sycamore tree on a swatch of grass. Katie has the marketing plan, a pile of other papers and a laptop computer.

Robbie and DIGGER COOTS, a burly, middle-aged man in blue overalls, walk by. Robbie and DIGGER hold fishing rods.

> KATIE
> Where do you think you're going?

ROBBIE

Down to the lake. To catch some fish.

KATIE

What about the business plan? There're a hundred things to do.

ROBBIE

I thought we were giving this up.

KATIE

No way! Get down to business.

ROBBIE

All this is going to lead to is stress. I've had my fill of it. I want to relax, enjoy life. The truth is I'm beginning to enjoy washing dishes and fixing things.

KATIE

You go ahead and go fishing if you want. You have to live with yourself.

Robbie and Digger head off.

Katie goes back to work at her laptop.

EXT. HIGHWAY ROADSIDE—DAY

Katie, thin and scarecrow-like SOURDOUGH SIMS and SISSY TAVELENE, a buxom, middle-aged blonde in tight jean shorts and low-cut blouse, nail "Pop's Diner" SIGNS to telephone polls.

EXT. MCBURGER PALACE—DAY

Katie puts paper "Pop's Diner" flyers under the windshield wipers of cars parked in the parking lot.

Tess passes out "Pop's Diner" flyers to PEOPLE leaving McBurger Palace.

INT. GAS STATION—DAY

Luther puts "Pop's Diner" flyers in the pamphlet rack by the cash register counter.

INT. WAL-MART—DAY

Sims, ballooned to hugely fat proportions, pulls out "Pop's Diner" leaflets concealed under a lumberjack shirt, and puts the leaflets in an aluminum leaflet rack.

EXT. MCBURGER PALACE—EVENING

Robbie waits outside the restaurant. Cars come and go in the parking lot and through the drive-in window.

Katie exits the restaurant door. Katie walks off down the road.

Robbie runs after her.

Robbie catches up with Katie.

ROBBIE

It's a great night, don't you want to take a
walk down by the pond?

KATIE

No, I have work to do.

ROBBIE

How about an ice cream cone?

KATIE

No.

ROBBIE

How about a movie?

KATIE

I told you, I have work to do.

ROBBIE

You're awfully rangly this evening.

KATIE

There's work to be done. Somebody's got to
do it. If you're not going to help, then I'll do
it myself.

Katie storms off.

EXT. THE OLD FISHING HOLE—DAY

Robbie, Digger and the dog sit on the bank of the lake. Their
fishing lines are in the water.

ROBBIE

I just don't understand women. Never did.
Never will.

DIGGER

They can be an independent lot, for sure. I
guess that's why I never tied the hitch.

Robbie's bobber dips and up and down.

DIGGER
(continuing)
You got a hit.

Robbie yanks the fishing pole.

ROBBIE

Lost it.

DIGGER

Oh, well, there'll be another one.

ROBBIE
(distractedly)
I'm not so sure.

DIGGER

Course there will. I've been fishing this hole
all my life. There's always another one.

ROBBIE

Oh, I didn't meant the fish.

> DIGGER

You're sweet on Kate.

> ROBBIE

More than sweet.

> DIGGER

Oh, I see; you got a case.

> ROBBIE

I just wish she'd see my view of things. I thought she did. Now she wants to get us back into the rat race.

> DIGGER

Anyway you look at it, life's a rat race.

Birds CHIRP in the trees.

> ROBBIE

No, I mean, look at this peaceful lake. The sky. The birds. Compare this to twelve telephone calls on waiting, running through airports, arguing with people, people trying to screw you, you trying to screw them back. There's no comparison.

> DIGGER

I wouldn't know.

> ROBBIE

Believe me. In the business world, Hell is other people.

INT. DINER—DAY

Mom serves a MAN and a WOMAN at the counter a plate of food and coffee. Pop is behind the counter.

Tyson, his rotund frame stuffed into a canvas, safari jacket with bulging pockets, and EARNEST JENKINS, an equally fat man in a polyester, plaid jacket and slacks, enter. Jenkins holds a long, rolled tube of paper in his hand.

Tyson and Jenkins squeeze into a booth by the window.

> MOM
> Howdy, Mr. Tyson. What'll you two gentlemen have?

> TYSON
> Give me some waffles, a double order of sausages, coffee, a sweet roll, and, say, you wouldn't have some of those french fries like they make out at McBurger Palace?

> MOM
> No, just hash browns.

> TYSON
> (disappointed)
> Hhmm. Well, give an order of them, too.

Mom scribbles the order on a little pad.

Mom turns to Jenkins.

MOM
And what'll you have?

JENKINS
The same.

Mom goes off.

TYSON
(addressing Pop)
You ought to get with the times, Pop. Those
McBurger fries are mighty good eating. No
wonder this place can't make a go of it.

POP
I'm not sure if those McBurger fries are even
made out of potatoes.

TYSON
Who cares? They taste mighty fine.

Tyson turns to Jenkins.

TYSON
(continuing)
Let's see what we got, Earnest.

Jenkins unrolls the paper tube. On the paper is an
architectural drawing of the interior of an ammo store.

Jenkins points to a feature on the paper.

JENKINS

See, we convert the counter to a showcase
for pistols, guns and knives. The wall behind
the counter is ripped out, and where the
kitchen is we put racks for the rifles and
shotguns.

Pop forlornly hands the plates of food to Mom through the
opening from the kitchen behind the counter.

Mom brings the plates of food to the booth. Mom puts the
plates on the perimeter of the paper.

Pop comes out of the kitchen. Pop refills the coffee pot
behind the counter.

Tyson wolfs down a large mouthful of waffle and sausage.

JENKINS
(continuing)
And over on that wall, we'll put some
stuffed animal heads. Like a deer and a bear.

TYSON
(talking while eating)
Hey, I got an idea? Why don't we stuff
Pop's head and mount it on the wall. As a
memento of the past?

Tyson LAUGHS, spewing bits of food over the table and the
architectural drawing.

Jenkins LAUGHS.

JENKINS
Now wouldn't that be something!

Pop goes back into the kitchen.

Mom brings the check to the booth and puts it on the table.

TYSON
Let's get going, Earnest. I want to go over to
the realty office.

Tyson picks up the check.

Tyson and Jenkins squiggle to get out of the booth.

Tyson and Jenkins can't budge.

Tyson and Jenkins are stuck in the booth, their large bellies
pressed firmly against the table top.

Mom looks at Tyson and Jenkins disdainfully. Mom goes
back into the kitchen.

Robbie, in dishwasher apron and rolled up shirt sleeves,
comes out of the kitchen.

Robbie goes to the booth and silently pulls the table way
forward, liberating Tyson and Jenkins.

ROBBIE
There you go, gentlemen.

Tyson goes to the register at the end of the counter and puts the check and some bills on the counter in front of Mom.

> TYSON
>
> Remember now, Mom, put some of those McBurger fries on the menu. They're mighty tasty!

Tyson CHORTLES, waves and exits with Jenkins.

Mom RINGS up the register, shaking her head.

INT. DINER—DAY

Robbie sits at the counter with a cup of coffee. Mom fixes a tray of pastries under the plastic cover of a tray on the counter.

Katie, her hair in a ponytail, enters with a pile of paper posters.

> KATIE
>
> Mom, have you seen Luther anywhere?

> MOM
>
> No, I guess he's at home.

Katie drops the posters on the counter next to Robbie.

> KATIE
>
> When you see him, tell him these posters have to be put up all over town.

                    ROBBIE
     Hi, Katie.

Katie ignores him.

                    KATIE
     See you later, Mom.

Katie exits.

Robbie gets up and follows her through the door.

EXT. STREET—CONTINUING

Katie walks rapidly down the street, her ponytail bobbing.

Robbie catches up with Katie.

                    ROBBIE
     Katie.

Katie continues to walk.

                    ROBBIE
                 (continuing)
     Katie.

Katie turns.

                    KATIE
     Yes? What is it?

ROBBIE

You haven't spoken to me for a week.

KATIE

So? What do we have to talk about?

ROBBIE

Us.

KATIE

What's this us? You won't help me, you
won't help Mom and Pop, you won't help
Tess and Luther. You won't help the town.
All you want to do is fish and wash dishes.
What kind of life is that!

ROBBIE

But . . .

Katie storms off.

EXT. COUNTRYSIDE—DAY

Robbie, holding a a brush and a child's plastic palate with
twelve different colors, stands in front of an easel before a
field of sunflowers.

The WATERCOLOR on the easel is half-finished. The
painting of the flowers is very crude and child-like.

INT. DINER—NIGHT

Light from the kitchen falls out onto the counter and tables in the empty, closed diner.

INT. DINER KITCHEN—NIGHT

Robbie washes a pile of pots, pans and dishes in the sink.

The dog lays on the floor at Robbie's feet, watching Robbie.

INT. SHED—NIGHT

Robbie is in bed. He reads an old ragged copy of <u>Sports Illustrated</u>. The dog is at bedside on the floor.

Thunder CRASHES and lightning FLASHES through the window.

EXT. SHED—NIGHT

A howling WIND BLOWS through the trees. RAIN falls in torrents.

INT. SHED—CONTINUING

The dog WHIMPERS, looking at Robbie with wide, forlorn eyes.

                    ROBBIE
          Some storm, huh. No night for neither man
          nor beast.

Robbie turns back to the magazine.

(S.O.) A POUNDING on the door.

Robbie gets up and opens the door.

Digger, in a poncho dripping with rain, stands in the doorway, WIND and RAIN howling about him outside.

> DIGGER
>
> Robbie, you got to come help. Katie's in a mess of trouble.

> ROBBIE
> (alarmed)
> What do you mean?

> DIGGER
>
> She was out putting up posters. Damn fool thing to do; everybody knew the storm was coming.

> ROBBIE
>
> So, what's the matter?

> DIGGER
>
> Rain loosened a sink hole. Ground collapsed under her. She fell in.

> ROBBIE
>
> My God! Let's go.

Robbie exits the shed, the dog in pursuit.

Robbie and Digger run down the street.

DIGGER

We called the state police but it'll be a while
before they get here.

EXT. SINK HOLE—NIGHT

Robbie and Digger arrive at the sink hole. The STORM is
unabating. Robbie's shirt and jeans are soaked through.
Water streams down Robbie's hair and face.

Pop Sims, Sissy and ORAM OGELTHORPE, the short,
balding proprietor of the hardware store, are gathered around
the hole.

Robbie goes to the edge.

Robbie's P.O.V.—

At the bottom of the muddy hole, twenty feet down, is Katie,
in her McBurger Palace uniform. Katie is drenched and
muddy up to her knees in brown, muddy water.

KATIE
(screaming hysterically)
Get me out of here!

ROBBIE
It'll be OK, Katie.

KATIE
No, not you! Somebody else get me out of
here!

Robbie steps back from the edge of the hole. Mud slides from the edge of the hole into the pit.

POP

> If this rain keeps up, the mud could collapse
> in on her and she'll be buried.

ROBBIE

> Get some rope from the hardware store. As
> long as you can. Break in if you have to.

OGELTHORPE

> No need. Got the key right here.

Ogelthorpe and Pop run off.

Robbie goes back to the edge of the hole.

ROBBIE

> Stay calm, Katie. I'll get you out.

KATIE

> (hysterical)
> No need to exert yourself. Why don't you go
> fishing? I'll take care of myself.

INT. HARDWARE STORE—NIGHT

Ogelthorpe and Pop grab a long coil of thick rope.

EXT. SINK HOLE

Katie's P.O.V.—

The muddy water is up to her waist. Thunder CRASHES and LIGHTNING FLASHES in the sky visible through the top of the hole.

Rain and mud fall into the hole on top of Katie.

Katie SCREAMS.

EXT. SINK HOLE—CONTINUING

Robbie peers down the hole.

> ROBBIE
> Hang on, Katie! We're getting a rope!

> KATIE
> You can go hang yourself with it!

Ogelthorpe and Pop run up with the coil of rope.

Robbie takes the rope and runs over to a nearby tree.

Robbie wraps the rope around the tree and ties the end of the rope in a secure knot.

Robbie drags the rope back to the edge of the sink hole.

Robbie throws the rope into the hole.

Robbie hands the length of rope to Ogelthorpe and Sims.

> ROBBIE
>
> I'm going down. If something happens. Be
> prepared to pull us up quickly. All of you.

Robbie lowers himself into the hole by the rope.

INT. SINK HOLE

Robbie lowers himself next to Katie.

> ROBBIE
>
> Grab hold of me Katie. I'll pull us out.

> KATIE
>
> (hysterically)
> Get away from me! Don't you have anything
> better to do!

Robbie grabs Katie, pulling her body to his chest, the rope on
the outside of Katie's back.

Robbie braces his feet on the slippery mud on the side of the
hole and clamps the rope in his hands.

> ROBBIE
>
> One way or the other, you're coming out of
> here.

Robbie, straining with all his might, climbs up the side of the
muddy hole with the rope, Katie against him.

EXT. SINK HOLE

Ogelthorpe, Sims, Sissy and Pop help pull Robbie and Katie out of the hole.

The dog watches them from the other side of the hole.

Robbie and Katie stand by the side of the hole, out of breath.

> ROBBIE
> If I lost you, I don't know what I would do.
> You're the best thing that ever happened to
> me. I love you.

Katie's eyes glisten.

> KATIE
> Oh, Robbie, I love you, too!

Robbie kisses Katie; they embrace and kiss.

Ogelthorpe, Sims, Sissy and Pop CHEER. The dog BARKS.

> ROBBIE
> I don't care about starting a chain of
> restaurants. But if that's what you want to
> do, I'll do it. I'll do anything for you.

INT. KATIE'S HOUSE—KITCHEN—DAY

Katie is on the phone at the kitchen table. Robbie reads the <u>Wall Street Journal</u>.

> KATIE
> Gail, are you still dating Tommy?

EXT. MANHATTAN SKYLINE—DAY

Establishing.

INT. GYM—CONTINUOUS

GAIL, in tights, is in a Lotus position, her legs crossed. Gail holds a mobile phone to her ear.

Around her are a DOZEN WOMEN, similarly attired, meditating in yoga positions. A turbaned Indian with a beard, clad in white pajamas, helps adjust the posture of a WOMAN standing on her head.

> GAIL
> Yes, can you believe it!

> INTERCUT AS NEEDED

> KATIE
> Is he still with Witherspoon, Drake and Temple?

> GAIL
> Oh, yes. And moving right up. They're even letting him do more than file SEC forms.

> KATIE
> Could you ask him if he could get a meeting with Witherspoon? I've got a great idea for a venture capitalist like him.

GAIL

I guess so.

KATIE

Thanks, Gail. You're a sweetheart. Let me know.

GAIL

OK. Bye.

INT. KATIE'S HOUSE—KITCHEN

KATIE

She'll do it.

ROBBIE

That's great! But how're we going to get there? Between us we don't have enough money for airfare for one. Let alone a hotel room.

KATIE

We'll drive!

ROBBIE

Drive what?

KATIE

The old car. Mom and Dad's. It's still in the garage.

ROBBIE

And clothes? Look at me.

EXT. WAL-MART—DAY

Establishing.

INT. WAL-MART—MEN'S CLOTHING DEPARTMENT

Robbie tries on different suits.

Katie nixes them.

Then Robbie finds a dark blue, three-piece suit.

Katie gives Robbie the thumbs up.

INT. WAL-MART—WOMENS' CLOTHING SECTION

Katie tries on different outfits.

Robbie nixes them.

Then Katie finds a gray, pin-striped business suit and light blue blouse.

Robbie gives Katie thumbs up.

INT. BARBERSHOP—DAY

Robbie's in the barber chair. The barber, 90-years-old, slowly trims Robbie's hair.

Katie enters. Katie yanks Robbie out of the chair.

INT. BEAUTY SALON—DAY

Robbie is in the barber chair. A middle-aged WOMAN in a smock cuts Robbie's hair with a scissors.

Katie holds in front of the woman a magazine open to a full-page photo of a young man with a great-looking, clean haircut.

EXT. DINER—DAY

A red, 1970 Chevrolet is in the street in front of the diner.

Robbie's behind the wheel; Katie in the seat beside him.

Pop and Mom, Luther, Tess, Digger, Sissy and Sims stand on the sidewalk beside the car.

The group waves goodbye.

> MOM
> Don't forget to send us a postcard!

The car drives off.

EXT. HIGHWAY—DAY

Wheat fields.

INT. CAR—DAY

Robbie behind the wheel.

DISSOLVE TO:

INT. CAR—NIGHT

Katie behind the wheel.

DISSOLVE TO:

EXT. HIGHWAY—DAY

Industrial parks, warehouses.

INT. CAR—DAY

Robbie behind the wheel.

EXT. MANHATTAN SKYLINE—DAY

Establishing.

EXT. BRIDGE—DAY

The car drives across the George Washington Bridge.

EXT. MANHATTAN STREET—DAY

The car pulls into the entrance of a parking lot.

SIGN—PARKING RATES: "$1 PER 20 MINUTES. MAXIMUM $24."

The car backs out of the entrance and slowly drives down the street.

EXT./INT. CAR

A bum, PATRICK O'ROURKE, carries a beat-up, cardboard SIGN around his neck that READS—"WILL WORK FOR FOOD."

Robbie sticks his out of the car window.

> ROBBIE
>
> Hey, can you drive?

> O'ROURKE
>
> Can I drive? Can I drive? You bet I can drive. That's what I did before I was laid off. I drove a moving van.

> ROBBIE
>
> Get in and drive this around for a while. Come back in two hours.

> O'ROURKE
>
> This some kind of trick?

> ROBBIE
>
> No. You look like an honest man.

> O'ROURKE
>
> Am I on TV?

                    ROBBIE
        No. Drive around and I'll treat you to a nice
        hot meal.

Robbie and Katie get out of the car.

                    KATIE
                (to Robbie)
        Are you sure you want to do this? What if
        he takes off?

                    ROBBIE
        What choice do we have?

O'Rourke gets in the car.

                    ROBBIE
                (continuing)
        You got a name?

                    O'ROURKE
        Patrick O'Rourke.

                    ROBBIE
        OK, Patrick. We'll be back.

Robbie and Katie dash through the door of a skyscraper,
briefcases in hand.

INT. SKYSCRAPER LOBBY—DAY

Robbie and Katie dash through the lobby.

ROBBIE
Come on, we've got about three minutes.

Robbie and Katie dash into the elevator.

INT. ELEVATOR—CONTINUING

Robbie and Katie smooth their clothing out—to the consternation and annoyance of the other PEOPLE in the elevator.

INT. SKYSCRAPER CORRIDOR—CONTINUING

Robbie and Katie walk out of the elevator.

Robbie and Katie smooth their hair in the shiny reflection of The closed, aluminum elevator door.

Robbie and Katie walk down the corridor.

A sign on a big glass door at the end of the corridor READS in gold lettering—"WITHERSPOON, DRAKE AND TEMPLE, INVESTMENT BANKERS."

INT. CONFERENCE ROOM—DAY

WENDEL WITHERSPOON, tall, lanky and in his 40's, and BART DRAKE, short, medium-built with black curly hair, also in his 40's, sit at a long, highly polished, wooden conference table.

Robbie gets up from his seat. A Wal-Mart tag hangs out of the back of Robbie's jacket.

Katie rips the tag off as Robbie moves forward to the front of the conference room. Katie hides the tag among the papers in front of her.

Robbie addresses Witherspoon and Drake from the front of the room at the head of the table.

ROBBIE
We would fill a missing niche in the trillion dollar restaurant industry. People want traditional good home cooked meals, but they don't want to cook at home. They want better than fast food, and they can't afford trendy nouveau cuisine. Pop's Diner is the answer.

WITHERSPOON
So, what do you propose?

ROBBIE
Katie?

Katie gets up and walks to the front of the room. Katie opens the briefcase she has with her and unfurls a map. Katie tapes the map to the wall.

KATIE
We plan to start in the Midwest, where our core marquee restaurant is. We plan to go head-to-head with McBurger Palace and the high—end haute cuisine restaurants. If we're successful in the midwest targets, we'll do an IPO to raise the cash for a national expansion. Of course, Witherspoon, Drake

and Temple would do the IPO. And you know what kinds of commissions and fees that could generate.

WITHERSPOON
Bart, what do you think?

DRAKE
Good idea. Sound business plan. Capable management.

WITHERSPOON
I think we can invest half a million in initial capital, but that's all. We'll monitor progress as you go along each quarter. If you meet your targets, we'll see about more financing.

Robbie and Katie look at one another.

ROBBIE
Can I confer with my partner?

WITHERSPOON
Sure.

ROBBIE
Excuse us for a moment.

Robbie and Katie go to the far end of the conference room.

KATIE
(whispering)
My goodness! A half-million.

> ROBBIE
>
> Don't say anything. Just do as I say. Shake
> your head back and forth.

Witherspoon's P.O.V.—Katie shakes her head back and forth.

> ROBBIE
> (continuing)
> Stamp your foot on the floor.

Witherspoon's P.O.V.—Katie stamps her foot on the floor.

Robbie puts his hands on Katie's shoulders.

> ROBBIE
> (continuing)
> Smile.

Katie smiles.

Robbie and Katie go back to Witherspoon and Drake.

> ROBBIE
> (continuing)
> We were looking for more. But we're capable
> of working on a shoestring. We'll take it.

Witherspoon and Drake relax and breathe out SIGHS of relief.

> DRAKE
> Our attorneys, Smoot, Hawley and Thatcher
> will draw up the papers. They'll be in
> contact.

Drake takes a large checkbook from the table and writes a check.

DRAKE
(continuing)
Until then, here's an initial check as a sign of good faith.

Drake hands the check to Robbie.

Robbie doesn't look at the check. Robbie confidently puts the check inside his jacket pocket.

ROBBIE
Of course.

WITHERSPOON
Now, if you'll excuse us, we've got another meeting.

ROBBIE
Of course.

KATIE
Of course.

Robbie and Katie shake hands with Witherspoon and Drake.

Robbie and Katie exit.

EXT. BANK—DAY

Robbie and Katie emerge from a bank onto Park Avenue.

Robbie and Katie give each other double high fives.

> ROBBIE
>
> Do you believe?

> KATIE
>
> No. But remember how it used to be. In those executive suites, there's no end to money, and baloney.

(O.S.) HONK! HONK! HONK!

Robbie and Katie turn and look.

Robbie and Katie's P.O.V.—

The Chevrolet is double-parked on the street with O'Rourke behind the wheel. O'Rourke waves.

Robbie and Katie jump into the car.

> O'ROURKE
>
> I've been driving in circles for the past two hours. I was starting to get dizzy. So how about that meal you promised?

> ROBBIE
>
> I've got better than that.

> O'ROURKE
>
> Uh, oh. I knew there was some kind of trick. What could be better than a nice juicy steak?

ROBBIE

You've proved yourself to be an honest man,
and a man of integrity. How would you like
a job?

O'ROURKE

A job? Sure!

ROBBIE

You'd work for us.

O'ROURKE

Doing what?

ROBBIE

Well, the first thing you could do is drive
us back to Iowa. Then, after that, they'll be
plenty.

O'ROURKE

Sure. Ok. It's a deal. Always wanted to see
America.

EXT. STREET

The car drives off.

INT. DINER—DAY

Katie is at the cash register, serving as hostess.

Mom's the waitress.

Pop cooks in the kitchen.

Robbie does the dishes.

INT. KATIE'S HOUSE—KITCHEN—NIGHT

Katie sits at the kitchen table, pouring over sheets of papers.

Robbie enters.

Robbie leans over the back of Katie's chair and kisses Katie on the cheek.

> ROBBIE
>
> Hi, honey.

> KATIE
>
> We're not going to make it.

Robbie gets a glass of milk from the refrigerator.

> ROBBIE
>
> What do you mean?

> KATIE
>
> If we keep going as we are, we won't meet the target set by Witherspoon.

> ROBBIE
>
> I thought we were doing OK. Pop's Diner has never been as busy.

KATIE

I know. But we've still got to get more customers in during the day. Breakfast is OK. Lunch could use some patrons. We've got to work on dinner. And how we do that, I don't know.

INT. KATIE'S HOUSE—BEDROOM—NIGHT

Robbie and Katie in bed. The window's open and a light breeze ruffles the window curtain. The light SOUNDS of INSECTS in the night suffuse the room. The room is lighted in gold by a table lamp on a night stand.

KATIE

We've only got so much to work with.

ROBBIE

No matter what happens, we've got each other. That means a lot.

Katie kisses him.

KATIE

Let's get some sleep. Tomorrow's another day.

Katie rolls over.

Robbie lays awake.

DISSOLVE TO:

Robbie tosses and turns. His eyes are open. He looks at the clock, which READS: "3 A.M."

Robbie looks over at Katie. Katie is fast asleep.

Robbie lays in bed with his eyes open.

> FROG (O.S.)
> BRRRUUUUPPPPPP!

Robbie stares at the ceiling.

> FROG (O.S.)
> BRRRUUUUUPPPPP!

Robbie shakes his head.

Robbie gets up and goes to the window. Robbie looks out the window.

Robbie's P.O.V.—The countryside illuminated in moonlight.

> FROG (O.S.)
> (continuing)
> BRRRRRUUUUUPPPPP!

Robbie turns to Katie and dives into bed.

> ROBBIE
> Katie! Wake up, wake up! I've got it!

Katie wakes in alarm.

> KATIE
>
> What's the matter!

> ROBBIE
>
> I've got it. An idea.

> KATIE
>
> (sleepily)
> What's that?

> ROBBIE
>
> We'll have a frog slog.

> KATIE
>
> A frog . . . what?

> ROBBIE
>
> A frog slog.

> KATIE
>
> (sleepily)
> A frog . . . oh well, whatever. Tell me about
> it in the morning.

Katie rolls over and goes back to sleep.

EXT. HIGHWAY—DAY

Cars speed down the road.

The cars pass roadside BILLBOARDS for gasoline, autos, TV sets, McBurger Palace.

Then a large sign that READS: "FROG DAYS IN VESTULIA. SPONSORED BY POP'S DINER. FROG SLOG AND JUMPING FROG CONTEST."

INT. POP'S HOUSE—DINNING ROOM—DAY

Luther and Tess are at the laptop computer.

Katie enters. Katie has a shoe box in her hands.

> KATIE
> Hi, guys. How are you doing?

> TESS
> We created the web site. How does this look?

COMPUTER TV MONITOR

A giant bullfrog jumps in the air over a pool of splashing water. "JUMP OVER TO VISTULIA FOR FROG DAYS. TICKETS AVAILABLE AT POP'S DINER."

> KATIE
> That looks great!

> LUTHER
> And we sent that same message to all travel
> agents in the United States.

Katie puts the shoe box on the table.

> KATIE

I brought you a present, Tess.

Katie takes the top off the shoe box.

INSIDE BOX—A FROG

> KATIE
> (continuing)

It's a female frog.

> TESS

She's so cute! Thanks, Katie.

Tess gives Katie a peck on the cheek.

> TESS
> (continuing)

I'm going to call her Lillian, after lily pads.

Mom enters.

> MOM

Katie, sorry to interrupt. But we need you over at the diner

> KATIE

What's the matter?

> MOM

Nothing. The phone's been ringing off the hook; people want to know about Frog

Days. We can't get anything else done other
than answer the phone.

EXT. DINER—DAY

PEOPLE line up outside.

The line goes down the street and around the corner.

Outside the diner, on the sidewalk, is a table.

A big sign to the side of the table READS: "REGISTER FOR
FROG DAYS."

More PEOPLE are lined up in front of the table. The line
goes down the street.

Tess and Luther are behind the table. A family of FOUR, a
man, woman, a little girl and boy stand in front of them.

> TESS
> The twelve biggest frogs caught in the Slog
> get to enter the Jumping Contest. You need
> to get your own container. All frogs are
> returned to the pond. You can't keep them.

INT. DINER—DAY

The diner is jammed pack to capacity.

Katie and O'Rourke dash about. Katie and O'Rourke get
plates of food from the counter and dash with them to the
CUSTOMERS in the booths.

Katie takes an order and YELLS it across the diner to Pop, wearing a chef's hat, who peers through the kitchen opening behind the counter.

KATIE

Two orders of meat loaf, mashed potatoes and green beans! One open-faced turkey sandwich, hold the fries!

Mom, in a gingham dress and new hairdo, is at the door with a reservation book in hand.

The FAMILY of FOUR from McBurger are at the front of the line of people at the door.

MOM

Schenkle. Party of four. It'll be about 20 minutes.

EXT. DINER—DAY

Across the street from the diner, a young female JOURNALIST with big, wide glasses, a notepad in hand, interviews Robbie and McBurger Palace regional sales manager ALFRED SLURP, a tall, slick man in a conservative, charcoal-gray business suit. An attaché case is at Slurp's feet.

ROBBIE

It's nice of you to come the whole way from Des Moines. I hope this won't take too long. A lot of dishes are stacking up over there.

SLURP

I've got all afternoon. My time is your time.

JOURNALIST

We're interested in this story because it goes against the grain of the current trends in eating outside the home. So, tell me, Mr. Slurp, how does the McBurger Palace chain view what appears to be a return to family-style cooking here in Vistulia?

SLURP

Many people these days are eager to find food solutions to their busy, fast-paced lives. McBurger Palace's 2,000 restaurants seek to provide an alternate feeding experience for these people.

JOURNALIST

Like what?

SLURP

Well, for example, a burger isn't exactly a barbecued chicken wing, now is it?

JOURNALIST

What are you trying to do at Pop's Diner, Mr. Armstrong?

ROBBIE

No offense intended here to Mr. Slurp, but Pop's is an integral part of the community. A friendly place where people can come, have a good, healthy meal and relate to one another. A McBurger Palace moment is just that. Nothing else. It's an abstraction.

JOURNALIST
What do you say to that, Mr. Slurp?

SLURP
McBurger Palace always tries to be good neighbors. We're good corporate citizens of the community, and we always will be.

JOURNALIST
So, you think the Frog Slog sponsored by Pop's Diner is a good thing?

SLURP
McBurger Palace is always for what's good for the community. So, yes, yes we are.

JOURNALIST
So, how much of McBurger Palace profits go back into the community?

Slurp smiles and puffs out his chest with an air of self—righteousness.

SLURP
McBurger Palace is proud to award a $25 scholarship to the high school graduate with the highest grades in the communities where we operate.

The journalist scribbles in her pad.

> JOURNALIST
> Uh, huh . . .

> ROBBIE
> I've got to go. Good luck with your story.

Robbie races off across the street toward the diner.

Slurp picks up the attaché case. Slurp opens the attaché case.

Slurp takes out a paper bag emblazoned with the McBurger Palace logo.

Slurp reaches in the bag and takes out a paper container of golden french fries.

Slurp holds the container of french fries out to the journalist.

> SLURP
> Have a fry, gal!

The journalist takes a fry and nibbles on it musingly.

INT. DINER—DAY

Robbie rushes through the door.

> MOM
> I washed some of your clothes for you, Robbie. They're hanging in the kitchen.

ROBBIE

Thanks, Mom.

MOM

This fell out of one of the pockets.

Mom hands Robbie a card.

Robbie looks at the card.

SKY'S BUSINESS CARD

EXT. POND—DAY

Luther and Digger stretch a big BANNER from one tree to another. The banner READS: "GREAT FROG SLOG."

DIGGER

Let's take a break. I got a jar of lemonade.

Digger and Luther go off to the rear of the pond, walking around its perimeter.

Digger and Luther settle down on a patch of grass behind a bush. Digger extracts a jug of lemonade from under the bush.

DIGGER
(continuing)

I'm going to catch me the biggest frog.

LUTHER

Yeah, sure.

Digger hands Luther the jug of lemonade.

> DIGGER
>
> No, I mean it. I've been studying this pond.
> I know just where the biggest one you've ever
> seen is right over under those big bulrushes.

The water of the pond under the bulrushes is flat and quiet, the water placid.

(O.S.) The ROAR of two motorcycles breaks the silence.

Digger and Luther peer out from behind the bushes.

Digger and Luther's P.O.V.—

Tyson and Chisolm shut off their motorcycles and walk to the edge of the pond.

Tyson holds a stick of dynamite in his hand and a radio—controlled timer in a white plastic box. Chisolm has a pair of waders on that reach up to his chest.

> TYSON
>
> Just as I thought. Not a soul around. They're
> all too busy at that two-bit diner.

BEHIND THE BUSH

> DIGGER
>
> Well, I'll be!

POND BANK

Tyson hands Chisolm the dynamite stick.

> TYSON
> (to Chisolm)
> You just get out there and put this baby deep
> down in the mud under one of those lily
> pads out there.

> CHISOLM
> OK, boss.

Tyson holds up the plastic box that is the radio transmitter.

> TYSON
> Right before this idiotic slog, or whatever it's
> called, starts, I press the button. There isn't
> going to be a slog. Because there aren't going
> to be any frogs. Now get out there, you hear!

Chisolm wades into the pond.

Tyson LIGHTS a cigar with a wooden match.

Chisolm is in the middle of the pond, surrounded by lily
pads.

> CHISOLM
> (yelling)
> Here OK?

                    TYSON
                 (yelling back)
            That's fine!

Chisolm bends down below the water line with the dynamite. When Chisolm gets up, the dynamite stick is not in his hand.

Tyson puffs on his cigar, smiling.

Chisolm wades out of the pond.

                    TYSON
                 (continuing)
            Let's get out of here.

Tyson and Chisolm get on their motorcycles and START them.

Tyson throws his cigar butt on the still pond.

The cigar butt lands on the tranquil water next to a lily pad.

Tyson and Chisolm REV their motorcycles and ROAR off.

BUSH

Luther and Digger emerge.

                    DIGGER
            They're planning to blow up the pond and
            kill the frogs!

LUTHER

We should get Robbie and tell him!

DIGGER

No, no need to bother Robbie. He and Katie and Mom and Pop got enough on their hands with that crowd at the diner.

LUTHER

What are we going to do?

DIGGER

Know how to swim?

LUTHER

Course.

DIGGER

I'll tell you what then. Go out to the center of the pond where they put that stick of dynamite. Dive down, find it and pull it out of the mud.

LUTHER

Do you think I can do that?

DIGGER

Sure. I'll keep my eye on you.

POND BANK

Digger and Luther are the edge of the pond.

> DIGGER
> (continuing; to Luther)
> Take off your shoes.

Luther sits on the ground and takes off his shoes.

> DIGGER
> (continuing)
> The water'll probably go up to your neck, where you're going out there. When you get to the spot, dive under the water and get the dynamite stick. You should be able to feel it with your hands.

> LUTHER
> Maybe you should do this.

> DIGGER
> Would if I could. Truth is, I don't know how to swim.

Luther wades into the pond.

Luther gets to the center at the edge of a group of lily pads. The water is up to Luther's chin.

POND BANK

Digger follows Luther's progress with his finger.

> DIGGER
> (continuing; yelling)
> There! There!

POND

Luther submerges himself.

POND BANK

Digger wrings his hands.

POND

The water of the pond by the lily pads is tranquil. Luther is out of sight underwater.

POND BANK

Digger worriedly takes one of his shoes off while he keeps his eyes on the center of the pond.

POND

Still no sign of Luther. The water is unruffled.

POND BANK

Digger hurriedly takes off the other shoe.

Digger runs into the pond.

POND

Luther surfaces like a rising dolphin, splashing water all around him.

Luther holds up the stick of dynamite in his hand.

Luther wades toward Digger.

Digger helps Luther out of the water. Luther is covered in mud.

> DIGGER
> (continuing)
> You had me worried for a moment!

> LUTHER
> (smiling)
> After that, I know where to catch the biggest frog!

Digger rubs Luther's hair.

> DIGGER
> (laughing)
> Will see about that! I still got my eye on that big one over there.

> LUTHER
> What're we going to do now?

> DIGGER
> First, we going to go home and get you cleaned up. Then, I got an idea.

EXT. POND—EVENING

FAMILIES, MEN, WOMEN AND CHILDREN line up at the front of the pond. They carry glass mason jars, tin cans and empty cardboard milk containers. The BRRRUUUPPPP of frogs is heavy in the air.

Robbie and Tess sit at a table with a butcher scale and a measuring tape on it.

Katie walks up and down in front of the crowd of several hundred. Katie is in jeans and a sweat shirt, and she has a clipboard with a paper on it her hand. A whistle on a lanyard is around her neck.

> KATIE
>
> The slog will be one half-hour long. We don't want it any longer because we don't want to do any permanent damage to the pond. One frog per person. So when you get yours, please get out of the pond and take it over to the weighing station. The top twelve get to be in the Jumping Frog contest tomorrow. All other frogs caught tonight will be returned to the pond.

EXT. ROADSIDE BAR—EVENING

Two Harley hog motorcycles are parked in front by the road. LIGHT streams from the window out onto the roadside. LOUD country and western MUSIC wails from a juke box inside, the music spilling out into the night.

Tyson and Chisolm are propped on stools at the bar. The bar is empty but for a BARTENDER.

Tyson and Chisolm have empty shot glasses and cans of beer in front of them.

> TYSON
> (in good humored drunken fellowship)
> So old George Fenstermacher goes out duck hunting with Ennis Shriver. A bunch of ducks goes overhead and old George takes a potshot at them.

Tyson signals to the bartender.

> TYSON
> (continuing)
> Give us another round, will you, Pete?

EXT. ROADSIDE BAR—NIGHT

Digger and Luther, hunched over, run from the side of the bar to the two Harley hogs.

Digger shoves the dynamite stick up the tail pipe of Tyson's Harley hog.

> DIGGER
> This'll teach them.

Digger and Luther, crouching, run off.

INT. BAR

The bartender comes over with a bottle of brown rye whisky and pours the whisky from the bottle into Tyson and Chisolm's shot glasses.

CHISOLM

So what happened?

Tyson takes a hearty slug of whisky and knocks it back.

TYSON

So, oh yeah. One of them ducks fell down dead. Ennis goes over and looks at the duck, and says to Old George, "that was a waste of ammunition to shoot the duck. The fall alone would have killed him."

Tyson breaks out into a HUGE LAUGH, beaming.

Tyson gulps back the remainder of his glass of whisky.

TYSON

(continuing; laughing)
The fall alone would have killed him! Get it?
The fall alone would have killed him!

CHISOLM

Ain't that the truth.

Tyson quaffs some beer from the beer can.

TYSON

Say, what time is it?

Chisolm looks at the watch on his wrist.

CHISOLM

Six o'clock.

TYSON

Oh, hell, got so carried away, I almost forgot about those stupid frogs.

BARTENDER

Everyone's going to the Frog Slog tonight. Rather catch frogs than drink good whisky.

Tyson takes the radio-controlled plastic detonator out of his pocket.

TYSON

We'll just see about that!

Tyson presses the button on the transmitter.

(O.S.)A DEAFENING EXPLOSION.

C.U. Tyson's face, a deep furrow on his brow.

EXT. POND—NIGHT

The PIERCING SHRIEK of a whistle as two hundred, men, women and children run into the pond, jars and canisters aloft.

A FAT MAN grabs a FROG on a lily pad but the frog jumps away. The fat man falls face down in the pond.

A WOMAN holds a FROG in one hand, a glass jar in the other hand. The frog squiggles away.

A LITTLE BOY stuffs a FROG into pants pocket.

EXT. POND—TABLE—CONTINUING

A TEENAGE GIRL, an empty glass mason jar in her hand, and her MOTHER place a FROG on the butcher scale.

Tess holds the frog on the scale. Tess looks at the weight bar.

TESS

Three quarters of a pound.

Katie scribbles with a pencil on her clipboard.

Robbie measures the frog with the tape measure.

ROBBIE

Ten inches.

INT. KATIE'S HOUSE—KITCHEN—NIGHT

Katie's at the range. A coffee pot is on a burner.

Katie and Robbie are drenched. Katie's face is smudged with mud. Robbie has a big towel in his hands.

KATIE

Coffee's on. It'll warm us up.

Robbie dries Katie's hair and face with the towel. Some mud smudges remain on Katie's face.

ROBBIE
(giggling)
I don't know when I ever had such fun!

Katie takes the towel and dries Robbie's hair.

KATIE
(giggling)
Nor do I.

Robbie goes to the refrigerator.

Robbie opens the refrigerator door and looks in.

ROBBIE
I'm hungry. Want to try some Mississippi Mud Pie? I'm working on a new version.

KATIE
So that's why the kitchen was a mess when I got home.

ROBBIE
Now, now. I'm experimenting. I've added more chocolate. In fact, a whole lot more chocolate.

Robbie takes a plate out of the refrigerator upon which sits a thick, dark, chocolate pie.

Robbie puts the pie on the table. He puts a plate on the table with two forks.

Katie sits down at the table.

Robbie takes the coffee pot off the stove, gets two cups from the cupboard and puts the coffee pot and cups on the table.

Robbie pulls over a chair and sits down next to Katie.

Robbie dips his finger into the pie.

> ROBBIE
> (continuing)
> Go ahead. A taste.

Katie licks the pie off Robbie's finger.

> KATIE
> Delicious. A sure winner. It'll go great with Pop's coffee.

> ROBBIE
> You sure look cute with mud on your face.

> KATIE
> How come you don't have any mud on you?

> ROBBIE
> I'm not a child.

Katie puts her hand in the pie and scoops out a handful of the thick, viscous pie.

                              KATIE
                          (giggling)
            Oh, yes you are, Robbie Armstrong. You're a
            child at heart!

Katie flings the handful of pie at Robbie's face.

Robbie jumps up.

                              ROBBIE
            Food fight!

Robbie grabs a handful of pie and flings it at Katie.

Katie grabs more pie and throws it back at Robbie. Katie gets
up and runs to the back of the kitchen.

Robbie picks up the pie and chases after Katie.

Katie's back is to the kitchen counter.

Robbie flings a handful of pie at Katie and then another.

                              KATIE
                          (giggling)
            Stop! Stop! Enough! I give up!

Katie and Robbie's hair and faces are covered with the mud
pie.

Robbie takes Katie in his arms. Katie and Robbie kiss
through the pie on their faces.

KATIE
(continuing; giggling)
Like I said. Delicious.

ROBBIE
Oh, how I do love you!

EXT. TOWN STREET—DAY

Both sides of the main street are jam-packed with PEOPLE.
In the center of the street, several large circles, like a bull's-
eye, have been drawn in white chalk.

A sign over Pop's Diner READS: "JUMPING FROG
CONTEST." To the side of the diner, on the sidewalk,
is a chalk board on an easel with the names of the frog
contestants CHALKED in:
"Hopalong Cassidy," "Bud Wiser," "Jumpin' Jim," "Fred,"
"The Amphibinator," "Big, Green and Ugly."

Robbie is at the center of the circle with a LITTLE GIRL,
who holds a large BULLFROG in her hands.

Robbie holds a bullhorn in his hand. Robbie yells into the
bullhorn to the crowd.

ROBBIE
Ladies and gentlemen! "Jumpin' Jim."

A bus comes rolling down the street and stops just short of
the circle.

Skye comes out of the door of the "Hounds of Hades" bus onto the street. Skye waves to Robbie.

> SKYE
> (hollering)
> Wouldn't miss this for the world! You're my good luck charm, Mate! Where can we set up?

> ROBBIE
> Over there. On the sidewalk, to the side of the diner where the scoreboard is.

Louie and Stanley jump out of the bus. They unload two guitars, an amplifier and a drum set.

The little girl sets her frog down in the center circle.

The frog sits there.

The little girl gives the frog a poke with her finger.

The frog jumps the length of two circles.

The CROWD CHEERS.

Katie CHEERS.

Digger CHEERS.

SIDEWALK PODIUM

Skye and the band strike up their guitars and drums. They play a rock version of "Froggy Went 'A Court'n".

EXT. TOWN ALLEY—DAY

Tyson holds a large cigar box in his hand. Chisolm joins Tyson.

> TYSON
>> Take a look at this?

Tyson opens the cigar box.

BOX

Inside is MAX, the biggest BULLFROG ever seen. The frog is muscular, with a huge, barrel chest and solid pecs.

> TYSON
>> (continuing)
>> Meet Max. Specially bred genetically for such occasions.

Chisolm holds a hypodermic syringe in his hand.

> CHISOLM
>> Got this from the vet. Those Olympic runners use testosterone. One shot of this and Max here'll jump to the moon.

Chisolm injects Max with the hypodermic.

EXT. STREET

A MAN in overalls puts a BULLFROG down in the center of the circle.

The band PLAYS.

The frog jumps up in the air and lands back in the circle.

The man walks away dejectedly.

Katie writes on the chalk board.

A YOUNGSTER puts a FROG down in the circle.

The frog jumps to the last circle.

The crowd cheers. The band PLAYS.

Katie writes on the chalk board.

Robbie bellows through the bullhorn to the crowd.

> ROBBIE
>
> That's it folks. We'll have the winner's ceremony in a minute as soon as the judges tally up the score. Looks like we have some strong competition between "Big, Green and Ugly," and "The Amphibinator."

Tyson steps forward with the cigar box in hand.

The top of the cigar box bounces up and down.

TYSON

Not so fast, we have one more contender.

ROBBIE

Is that frog registered? We didn't see you at the pond last night.

TYSON

Oh, I was there. Guess you just didn't see me. You going to let me race my frog, or do I scream foul?

Robbie looks to Katie.

ROBBIE

What do we do?

KATIE

Oh, let him race his dumb frog. It can't be much of anything. And then maybe he'll go away and leave us alone.

ROBBIE

OK. I guess no harm done.

Robbie looks to Tyson.

ROBBIE
(continuing)
OK. Enter your frog into the arena.

Tyson steps to the center circle, a wide grin on his face.

Tyson sets the cigar box on the ground.

Tyson takes out Max.

Tyson places Max in the center circle.

The crowd GASPS.

> KATIE

Oh, my God!

Max STOMPS the ground with his webbed feet.

> TYSON

Watch this!

Tyson steps back.

Tess is on the curb of the sidewalk, at the front of the crowd, with her frog LILLIAN. Tess holds Lillian on a tiny leash. Lillian is in a little dress.

Max's P.O.V.—Lillian bats her eyelashes.

Max's eyes widen. The pupils of Max's eyes turn into pinwheels. Max's muscles inflate to a huge size. Max's long, drooling tongue drops to his bulging chest.

Lillian slips off the little leash. Lillian hops off toward the pond.

Max bounds up in the air and hops after Lillian in mad, amorous pursuit.

TYSON
(continuing)
Get back here!

Tyson chases after Max.

EXT. MANHATTAN SKYLINE—DAY

Establishing. An airplane flies over city.

EXT. MANHATTAN—OFFICE—DAY

A SIGN in gold lettering on a big glass door at the end of the corridor reads: "Witherspoon, Drake and Temple, Investment Bankers."

Witherspoon looks through a binder of papers.

WITHERSPOON
These numbers look fantastic.

DRAKE
Great marketing, financial savvy.

WITHERSPOON
Not to mention industriousness of the work ethic and spirit. We like that.

ROBBIE
So, you'll finance the expansion?

> WITHERSPOON
>
> You bet. Pop's Diner chain is going to be a great success.

> DRAKE
>
> We're going to get an IPO ready. If that's OK with you.

Robbie looks at Katie.

Katie smiles.

> ROBBIE
>
> You bet!

EXT. CINCINNATI—DAY

Establishing.

EXT. CINCINNATTI—A POP'S DINER—DAY

A long line of PEOPLE wait to get in the brand new, wood and brick restaurant, which has the "Pop's Diner" SIGN on its roof.

EXT. RALEIGH, NORTH CAROLINA—DAY

Establishing.

EXT. RALEIGH—A POP'S DINER—DAY

SIGN in window: "Mississippi Mud Pie, All You can Eat $1.95"

The CAMERA pulls back to show a long line outside a newly constructed "Pop's Diner."

INT. IOWA—TOWN—OFFICE—DAY

Robbie, Katie, Witherspoon and O'Rourke look over architectural drawings in a modern business office.

INT. NEW YORK STOCK EXCHANGE—DAY

OVERVIEW of exchange trading floor with the HUBBUB and HUSTLE and BUSTLE of stock traders.

STOCK TICKER

Electronic symbols flash by. The symbol PD 25 goes by amidst GM 36 INTEL 54 MRK 48 and then again PD 30 among MRK 80 NKE 22 MCRSFT 42 and again PD 38 amidst AHP 73 Cisco 54 WalMart 65.

EXT. TRAIN STATION CAFÉ—MORNING

Sam, in sweat shirt and baseball jacket, jeans and sneakers with a stubble of beard, reads the <u>Wall Street Journal</u>.

Willy, Walter, Brad and Charley sip coffee from white styrofoam cups and read newspapers.

> CHARLEY
> I see where Pop's Diner is up another point today.

                    WALTER

Should be paying a dividend one of these
days.

                    BRAD

Let's buy some.

                    WILLY

Sure, why not. Robbie could use some
support.

EXT. MANHATTAN SKYLINE—DAY

Establishing.

INT. MANHATTAN OFFICE—DAY

The board room of Witherspoon, Drake. A dozen BOARD
MEMBERS, including Mom and Pop, Drake, Witherspoon
and GAVIN RUMPLEPORT, wearing a gray three-piece suit
and pocket watch over his rotund girth, sit around a large
conference table.

Robbie and Katie stand at the front of the table. A screen with
a slide of a financial GRAPH is next to Robbie.

                  WITHERSPOON

These numbers are impressive. Yet, your
administrative costs are high. If you could
cut them, we'd make more profit, and the
stock would go even higher.

ROBBIE

That's true. But we've decided to make the restaurants just as profitable as they need to be, without gouging customers to make higher profits.

BOARD MEMBER

What's the matter with that?

ROBBIE

A lot. The reason why people like to eat at Pop's Diner is because it's an all-American, family and community-oriented place. They trust us to do the right thing. That's the secret to Pop's Diner's success.

BOARD MEMBER

It'll only be a success as long as we have the capital to grow and add more restaurants.

KATIE

Big and large doesn't mean better. The world is already too full of donut, burger, chicken and pizza chains. They're all the same.

ROBBIE

Our idea is to really give back to the community. We give a lot of money to good local charities. We give full, four-year scholarships to graduating high school seniors. We support all the local sports teams, hire the handicapped and minorities. They're all part of the community.

KATIE

We use only safe, environmentally sound, recyclable products. We only use healthy food ingredients. We contribute and deliver free food to elderly shut-ins, hospitals and nursing homes, and shelters for the poor and homeless.

ROBBIE

We don't want to be profitable just to be profitable. There's more to life than that.

BOARD MEMBER

I'm not sure I can agree with that.

RUMPLEPORT

You've been successful to this point. But with that kind of attitude, young man, we're not going to get very far. Maybe it's time for new management.

ROBBIE

When the numbers get in the way of people, don't you think that's the time to reevaluate your priorities?

RUMPLEPORT

I think you and I have what is called a difference of philosophy.

WITHERSPOON

You've given us a great deal to think about, Robbie. Let's adjourn and we'll get back to you.

Robbie and Katie exit.

ROBBIE

I don't like the looks of this.

KATIE

They're just doing what they're suppose to do. Watch over things.

RICHIE

Maybe so. But I once got sandbagged by old man Stinson after the Tungstron merger. I don't want it to happen again.

Katie kisses Robbie.

KATIE

You worry too much.

EXT. MANHATTAN—WALDORF ASTORIA HOTEL —AFTERNOON

INT. HOTEL—ROBBIE AND KATIE'S SUITE

Robbie and Katie work at a desk in the drawing room of the suite.

(O.S.) The doorbell rings.

Robbie goes to the door and opens it.

Mom and Pop are at the door.

> ROBBIE
>> Come on in.

Mom and Pop enter.

Mom and Pop take a seat on the couch.

Robbie and Katie sit down in chairs opposite them.

> ROBBIE
>> (continuing)
>> So how did the rest of the board meeting go?

> POP
> Not well. That Rumpleport is as big a scalawag as Tyson ever was. Bigger.

> KATIE
> I knew we should never had anything to do with him. His company has the worst minority hiring record around. And his salary's bloated beyond reason with cash and stock options.

> ROBBIE
> Witherspoon said a couple of corporate titans like Rumpleport on the board would go over big on Wall Street.

KATIE

Little did we know then. We were just innocents. We found out about him too late. It was a big mistake.

MOM

He's got the others all fired up about hiring new management.

POP

We tried to explain to them, but they wouldn't listen. Witherspoon and Drake are sympathetic to what we're doing, but the others are just a greedy lot.

ROBBIE

If what you say is correct, the board's split. Let me call Witherspoon.

Robbie walks over to the desk and picks up the phone.

EXT. MANHATTAN STEAK HOUSE—NIGHT

Establishing.

INT. STEAK HOUSE

Robbie, Witherspoon and Rumpleport are in a booth. Rumpleport drinks a clear martini from a large widestemmed glass. Robbie and Witherspoon sip red wine from wine goblets.

RUMPLEPORT

Now this is what I call living. Some people might like Pop's Diner, but this is what I call home.

A WAITER brings plates of food. The waiter puts a huge, thick, double Porterhouse steak and immense baked potato in front of Witherspoon. The waiter puts salads in front of Robbie and Witherspoon.

RUMPLEPORT
(continuing; to the waiter)
I'll have another martini. Make it a double.

Rumpleport digs into the steak with his knife and fork.

ROBBIE

To continue what we were saying. Mr. Rumpleport, can't you see that Pop's Diner is an idea whose time has come. America's changing. Back to old, traditional values. Pop's Diner is part of that change.

RUMPLEPORT

You talk about tradition, young man. Capitalism is America's tradition. And profit—the most profit—is the soul of Capitalism.

ROBBIE

Is there no middle ground?

RUMPLEPORT
Not when it comes to money.

WITHERSPOON
So you're determined to bring in new management?

RUMPLEPORT
Yes. And the sooner the better. I plan to ask for a vote of the board when we reconvene tomorrow. I've already sounded out the other board members and I got most of the votes. Didn't expect Mom and Pop to vote with me, anyway.

Robbie and Witherspoon look at one another.

RUMPLEPORT
(continuing)
You're not eating your dinners.

ROBBIE
Suddenly, I'm not very hungry.

RUMPLEPORT
Damn fine steak! Always come here when I'm in town.

Robbie gets up.

ROBBIE
You'll have to excuse me. I've got a lot of work to do.

Robbie exits, leaving Rumpleport chewing a big mouthful of steak, and Witherspoon abstractedly swirling wine in his wine glass.

INT. HOTEL SUITE—NIGHT

Robbie and Katie are collapsed in chairs.

> ROBBIE
>
> He's determined to do it.

> KATIE
>
> I can't believe it! After all this work. From where we started. It's criminal.

> ROBBIE
>
> Don't say I never warned you. The shareholders are the owners and the owners elect the board. I needn't remind you that the shareholders are only as good as today. They're never around for tomorrow. In one day and out tomorrow. That's their motto. And the bigger they are, the faster they're in and out.

> KATIE
>
> Now you're blaming me.

> ROBBIE
>
> No. No, I'm not. The whole system's rotten.

> KATIE
>
> No. The system's not rotten. It's the people who're entrusted to run the system.

ROBBIE

Yeah, you're right.

KATIE

So, what do we do now?

ROBBIE

Back to washing dishes and slinging burgers
and fries at McBurger Palace.

KATIE

Oh, Robbie.

Robbie and Katie embrace.

INT. OFFICE BUILDING—MORNING

Robbie and Katie sit in chairs in the lobby outside the
conference room. Robbie reads the <u>Wall Street Journal</u>. Katie
works on a Palm Pilot hand-held computer.

The door to the conference room opens.

Witherspoon enters the lobby.

ROBBIE

Well, so that's it, huh?

WITHERSPOON

No. Quite the contrary. You're in.
Rumpleport's out. He's resigning from he
board.

Robbie and Katie jump to their feet.

> ### ROBBIE
>
> What!

Mom and Pop stand at the doorway to the conference room.

> ### WITHERSPOON
>
> Yes. A dramatic and quite unexpected turn of events. Mom and Pop told the board that without you and Katie they would not let the company use "Pop's Diner" as a trademark. And without that, the company's nothing. Mom and Pop own the tradename. They never gave it up. The board has seen the wisdom of their ways.

Mom and Pop smile broadly.

Katie rushes over to Mom and Pop, and kisses each.

> ### POP
>
> Robbie, I told you way back when you put on that first can of paint on the wall, I'd pay you back.

> ### ROBBIE
>
> Pop, you're quite a man! And, Mom, you're quite a women.

Robbie gives Mom and Pop a hug.

EXT. TOWN—DAY

A large, sleek, twenty-story glass and aluminum skyscraper looms over the prairie and the little town.

Atop the gleaming edifice is a big SIGN with the Pop's Diner logo: a "PD" with a frog jumping frog over the initials.

Fountains spew water in front of the entranceway, where a large pond with water lilies sits.

MEN and WOMEN in business attire walk in and out of the front door.

INT. BUILDING LOBBY—DAY

A TOUR GUIDE, a young woman in her early 20's, shows a group of school CHILDREN around the lobby displays.

The guide stops in front of a portrait of Pop.

> TOUR GUIDE
> This is Pop. Pop's Diner is named after him. Pop
> worked hard all his life to create good food and
> a good, healthy atmosphere for the community.

C.U. Face of girl.

The guide moves to a portrait of Mom, hanging next to Pop's portrait.

> TOUR GUIDE
> (continuing)
> And this is Mom. She supported Pop all the
> way.

C.U. Face of boy.

The tour guide moves past a big photo of the Jumping Frog contest to a PLACARD on the wall.

> TOUR GUIDE
> (continuing)
> This is the company's mission statement.

The tour guide reads the placard.

> TOUR GUIDE
> (continuing)
> Pop's Diner is a business. But it does not put profit first. Our business is to provide a friendly eating establishment that is part of the community. If we do this, we will succeed as a business. If we have to put profits at the expense of our customers and everybody else who lives in the community, we should not be in business.

C.U. Faces of the children.

INT. BUILDING CORRIDOR—DAY

MEN and WOMEN in business attire walk briskly through the hallways.

Willy pushes a mail cart through the corridor. Willy passes by Brad, who is vacuuming the hallway carpet. Willy waves to Brad, who gives him the thumbs up.

Willy pushes the cart into a cubicle. Willy tosses a pack of mail on the table. Charley looks up.

> WILLY
>
> Today's mail. Needs to be distributed right away.

Charley takes the mail, and opens the top envelope.

> CHARLEY
>
> You bet!

INT. ROBBIE AND KATIE'S OFFICE—DAY

Robbie sits behind a desk. Katie sits at a desk opposite him, the desks abutting one another.

The phone on Robbie's desk BUZZES. Robbie punches the intercom button.

> SECRETARY
> (S.O.)
> Mr. O'Rourke, Vice President of Human Resources, is here.

> ROBBIE
>
> Send him in.

O'Rourke enters with a YOUNG MAN in his 30's.

> ### O'ROURKE
>
> I brought Johnny Hausfraus with me, Robbie. Remember, we were going to talk about his future.

Robbie and Katie look up.

> ### ROBBIE
>
> Let's sit over there. We'll be more comfortable.

Robbie, Katie, O'Rourke and Hausfraus sit down on a couch and chairs around a coffee table set to the side of the office.

> ### O'ROURKE
>
> We're reorganizing the purchasing department and consolidating a lot of positions. Johnny doesn't have as much seniority as Ted Hughes, so he's redundant.

> ### ROBBIE
>
> That shouldn't be a problem. Tell me, Johnny, what else are you good at?

> ### HAUFRAUS
>
> I've always been good at fixing things with my hands.

> ### ROBBIE
>
> Well, why don't you join the maintenance pool. We can always use another person to cut the grass.

Hausfraus is startled.

HAUFRAUS
I didn't get my MBA to cut grass.

ROBBIE
Of course not. That's not what I mean. Just until another job opens up that you're best qualified for. You'll be on the same salary and everything. The way we're growing, it shouldn't be too long before we're ready to add some more purchasing jobs. Right, Katie?

KATIE
Right.

HAUFRAUS
That sound like a good deal to me, Robbie. I can't thank you enough.

ROBBIE
You don't have to thank me. Everybody deserves a good turn now and then. Right, Katie?

KATIE
Right, Robbie.

O'Rourke and Hausfraus exit.

Robbie and Katie get up.

Robbie and Katie go the window. The lily pond on the plaza is visible through the wide glass window of the twentieth-floor office.

Robbie takes Katie in his arms.

Robbie and Katie embrace one another, all smiles.

                    KATIE
               (continuing)
          Decency. That's what it's all about.

                    ROBBIE
          Right, Katie.

EXT. MCBURGER PALACE—DAY

The parking lot is full of cars. Cars drive in and out of the drive-in window.

INT. MCBURGER PALACE

A FAMILY of five, MOTHER, FATHER, TWO YOUNGSTERS and a BABY in the mother's arms, stand at the counter behind an impatient line of CUSTOMERS.

                    FATHER
          Four burgers, one without ketchup, two
          fries, a vanilla milkshake and a strawberry
          milkshake and a Coke.

Tyson, sweating profusely behind the counter in a McBurger Palace uniform, types the order into the register. Tyson puts a plastic tray on the counter.

Tyson turns to the fast-food kitchen counter behind him.

Chisolm, in a McBurger Palace uniform, looks out through the opening.

> CHISOLM
> Was that three burgers and two fries, and three shakes, or four fries, three burgers and two shakes?

C.U. Tyson's brow furrows deeply, and his eyes cross.

FADE OUT:

THE END

AS CREDITS ROLL:

The song "Froggy Went 'A Court'n" PLAYS.

Disclaimer

AUTHOR

Jack Sholl is a former journalist and national editor with The Associated Press in New York and has worked on newspapers in New Jersey, Pennsylvania and Virginia. He is the author of a number of screenplays. He lives in Florida.

Editorial assistant: Veronica Rodriguez